www.BillieBBrownBooks.com

First American Edition 2023
Kane Miller, A Division of EDC Publishing

Original Title: *Billie's Special Stories*
Text copyright © 2016 Sally Rippin
Illustration copyright © 2016 Aki Fukuoka
Logo and design copyright © 2023 Hardie Grant Children's Publishing
First published in Australia by Hardie Grant Children's Publishing

All rights reserved, including the rights of reproduction
in whole or in part in any form.

For information contact:
Kane Miller, A Division of EDC Publishing
5402 S 122nd E Ave
Tulsa, OK 74146
www.kanemiller.com

Library of Congress Control Number: 2022945484
Printed and bound in the United States of America
1 2 3 4 5 6 7 8 9 10

ISBN: 978-1-68464-673-9

Billie's Special Stories

By Sally Rippin

Illustrated by Aki Fukuoka

A DIVISION OF EDC PUBLISHING

Contents

The Birthday Mix-up   1

The Big Sister   47

The Spotty Vacation   93

Billie B. Brown

The Birthday Mix-up

Chapter One

Billie B. Brown has ten invitations, two packages of balloons and one box of colored pencils. Do you know what the "B" in Billie B. Brown stands for?

Birthday.

Soon it will be Billie B. Brown's birthday. Isn't that exciting?

Billie is allowed to invite ten friends to her birthday party. This is very hard for Billie. There are twenty-one people in her class.

Billie wants to invite everyone, but her mom and dad say no, no and NO. They say ten noisy kids is plenty!

Billie is writing out her invitations. Jack is helping her decide who to invite to her party. Jack is Billie's best friend. He lives next door.

"I know!" Billie says, counting on her fingers. "There are exactly ten girls in our class, not including me. I will just invite the girls."

Jack frowns. "What about me?" he says.

"Oh," says Billie. "Of course."

Billie can't have a party without Jack!

"Well, maybe I won't invite Lola. She can be very annoying," Billie says. "How about nine girls and one boy?"

"Then Lola will be the only girl not invited," says Jack. "She won't like that. You'll hurt her feelings. And then she will be cross."

"You're right," says Billie.

"Maybe you should invite five girls and five boys?" Jack says. "That's fair."

"Good idea," says Billie. But it's still no good. Billie can only think of four boys she would like to invite. The other boys are just too **loud** and silly.

Oh dear. What a headache!

In the end, Billie decides to invite four boys and six girls.

Billie's mom writes everything on a piece of paper for Billie to copy. Her mom has to write quickly because Billie's baby brother, Noah, is hungry.

She writes:

> Saturday 4th April 12:30pm

Billie copies out all the invitations in colored pencil.

Here is one of Billie's invitations. Doesn't it look pretty?

PARTY

DEAR Poppy

PLEASE COME TO MY PARTY!

DATE: Saturday 4th ~~Afi~~ Aprill
TIME: 2:30 pm

FROM: Billie

Chapter Two

It is only five sleeps until Billie's party. She is very **excited**. Each day at school she checks that everyone is coming.

She has to whisper because she doesn't want the kids who aren't invited to feel left out.

"Are you coming to my party this Saturday?" Billie whispers to Poppy in class.

"Yes!" says Poppy.  "You've asked me ten times already, Billie."

"Are you getting me a present?" Billie asks.

"Billie, Poppy, no whispering in class," Ms. Walton says.

But Billie is so **excited** she can hardly keep still.

"My goodness," Ms. Walton says. "Did you eat jumping beans for breakfast, Billie?"

Ms. Walton makes Billie sit in the front row because she won't stop wriggling.

Every afternoon, Billie and Jack plan the games that they will play at Billie's party.

Billie has a special purple notebook where she writes down the list of games. Every day it changes.

Soon the list looks like this:

Every night, Billie asks her mom and dad how many sleeps until her party.

Every night her dad says, "One sleep less than the last time you asked, Billie."

"Don't worry, Billie," says her mom.

"Nobody is going to forget your party!"

But Billie lies in bed and **worries**.

What if they don't like the games? she thinks. *What if they don't like the food? What if the boys won't play with the girls? Or worst of all, what if... nobody comes?*

Chapter Three

Finally, it is Saturday. Billie rushes into her mom and dad's bedroom to see if they are awake. Billie's mom is sitting up feeding Noah.

Her dad is fast asleep. Billie jumps up and down on the bed to wake him.

Billie's dad rubs his eyes and yawns. Then he reaches under the bed and pulls out their birthday presents for Billie.

"Happy birthday, Billie!" her mom and dad say.

Billie opens her presents.
She has lots of lovely things.
She feels very lucky.

"Careful. Don't let Noah eat the paper!" her mom laughs.

Billie and Noah and their mom and dad have a big birthday cuddle on the bed.

Suddenly Billie sits up.

"What time is it?" she asks. "Is it nearly time for my party?"

"No, Billie, you have lots of time," her mom says. "Your friends aren't coming until twelve-thirty. Besides, you're going to Jack's for a special birthday breakfast, remember?"

"Twelve-thirty!" says Billie.

"That's ages away. Can I stay and play with Jack after breakfast?"

"OK," says Billie's mom. "Dad and I will get up soon and get ready for the party."

Billie puts on her bathrobe and runs downstairs and out into the backyard.

Then she squeezes through the hole in the fence into Jack's backyard.

Jack is sitting at his kitchen table. Billie knocks on the back door.

"Come in," says Jack's mom. "Happy birthday, Billie! We're making your favorite breakfast. Banana pancakes!"

"Yum!" says Billie.

Jack's mom makes a special plate of banana pancakes for Billie, with honey and sprinkles.

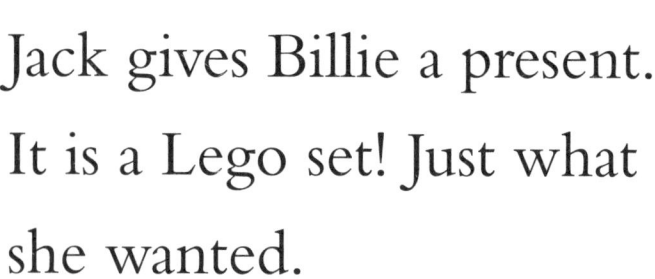

Jack gives Billie a present. It is a Lego set! Just what she wanted.

Billie and Jack sit in the family room and build a super-duper rocket ship.

Suddenly, Billie looks up. "What time is it?" she asks.

"Quarter past twelve," says Jack.

"Quick!" says Billie. "Everyone will be here soon! I have to get ready!"

Billie and Jack run next door to Billie's house. Billie goes upstairs and puts on her special party dress. Then she runs downstairs to the kitchen.

"Just in time!" says Billie's mom, smiling. "Everything is all ready for your party. Dad is just putting Noah to sleep.

Why don't you two sit on the front step to wait for everyone?"

"Yay!" say Billie and Jack. They run outside.

"What time is it?" says Billie.

Jack looks at his watch. "It's twelve-thirty," he says. "Anyone from now on is officially late!"

Billie giggles. "Don't worry, they'll be here soon. I checked with everyone and they all said they were coming."

Billie and Jack wait.

They wait and they wait and they wait.

But nobody comes.

Chapter Four

"What time is it now, Jack?" Billie asks in a little voice.

Jack looks worried. He looks down at his watch. "It's nearly one o'clock," he says.

Billie frowns. Her friends can't *all* be late.

Then she gets a funny feeling in her tummy. Her bottom lip begins to quiver and a big tear rolls down her face.

Nobody is coming to her birthday party!

Billie's mom comes out the front door. "My goodness!" she says. "They *are* late!"

Billie bursts into tears. "They're not coming!" she cries. "Nobody is coming to my birthday party! Nobody likes me!"

Billie's mom gives Billie a cuddle. "Did you give out all the invitations?" she asks.

"Yes!" sobs Billie.

"Did you check that everyone could make it?" says her mom.

"Yes!" sobs Billie. "Of course I did! Every day!"

Billie cries and cries. This is the worst birthday ever. Not one of her school friends is coming to her party.

"Are you sure you wrote the right date and time on the invitation?" Billie's mom asks. "Saturday the fourth of April at twelve-thirty?"

"Yes, yes and *yes*!" says Billie crying even louder.

But Jack frowns.
He looks like he is remembering something.

Can *you* remember?

Jack runs next door. A few minutes later, he runs back to Billie and her mom. He is waving the invitation in his hand and he has a huge smile on his face.

Do you know why?

Go back to have another look at the invitation.

That's right! Billie wrote down the wrong time on the invitations. Instead of twelve-thirty, she wrote two-thirty!

Billie's mom wrote so quickly that Billie couldn't read her writing properly.

Of course her friends are coming!

Billie wipes her eyes and laughs loudly. Jack and Billie's mom laugh too. What a mix-up!

Billie B. Brown

The Big Sister

Chapter One

Billie B. Brown has four baby jumpsuits, three tiny dresses and one big teddy bear. Do you know what the "B" in Billie B. Brown stands for?

Baby!

Billie's mom is having a baby. Billie is going to be a big sister!

These little clothes used to be Billie's. Aren't they tiny? They will be perfect for the new baby.

Billie is very **excited** about being a big sister.

She's going to give the baby her favorite teddy, Mr. Fred. Isn't that nice of her?

Billie has had Mr. Fred since she was a baby. But when the baby comes she won't need him anymore.

Today Billie is playing mommies and daddies with her best friend, Jack.

Jack lives next door.
Billie and Jack have
been friends since they
were little. They do
everything together.

Billie and Jack sit in the
fort they have made.
Billie squeezes Mr. Fred
into a pink dress.
He looks very funny.
Billie and Jack giggle.

Today it is Jack's turn to watch the baby while Billie goes off to work.

"I'm glad you're home," says Jack when Billie comes back. "Mr. Fred has been crying all day!"

Billie laughs and takes Mr. Fred. "I'm bored with playing mommies and daddies," she says. "Let's go and play soccer."

Jack and Billie run into the backyard to play.

Billie sits Mr. Fred on the grass to watch.

Oh dear. Look at those gray clouds.

Soon it starts to rain.

Billie and Jack run inside.
But they forget someone.

Poor Mr. Fred! He is
going to get very wet,
isn't he?

Chapter Two

That night, Billie's mom reads her a story in bed. It is about a mommy elephant and her baby. It is Billie's favorite book.

Suddenly Billie's mom stops reading. She gets a funny look on her face.

"Oh!" she says. "I think the baby is coming!"

She calls to Billie's dad.

Billie climbs out of bed and helps her mom downstairs. Billie's dad rushes around finding all the things they will need for the hospital.

Suddenly Billie gets a funny feeling in her tummy. "Can I come with you?" she says.

"No, sweetheart," says her dad. "Remember, we said that you will stay at Jack's house when the baby comes."

"How long will you be?" asks Billie, feeling **worried**.

"I don't know, Billie," says her mom.

She squeezes Billie's hand. "But just think – next time you see me, you will have a little baby brother or sister!"

But Billie has decided she doesn't want a silly old baby anymore.
She wants her mommy!
Billie scrunches up her face and tries not to cry.

"It's all right, Billie," says her dad gently.

Jack's mom comes over to pick up Billie. They watch Billie's mom and dad drive off.

Billie's mom blows a kiss, but Billie looks down at the ground. She doesn't want them to go without her.

Jack's mom gives Billie a cuddle. "I've made a bed for you in Jack's room," she says. They walk next door.

Jack is already asleep. His mom tucks Billie into the guest bed.

Jack's room looks strange in the dark. Billie wishes she was back in her own bed.

Suddenly she sits up.

"Mr. Fred!" she whispers. "I need Mr. Fred!"

"Oh dear. We'll get him tomorrow," says Jack's mom.

"How about you sleep with one of Jack's toys tonight?"

Jack's mom gives Billie a big blue teddy bear.
He is very soft and cuddly.
But he's not like Mr. Fred.

Billie lies in the dark.
Her tummy is curling up with **worry**.

She can't remember where she put Mr. Fred!

You remember where he is though, don't you?

Chapter Three

The next day, Billie has breakfast with Jack's family. But she doesn't feel very hungry.

Just then there is a knock on the door. It's Billie's dad!

"Billie!" he says excitedly. "Guess what? You have a baby brother!"

"A brother?" Billie says, frowning. "But I wanted a sister! Who will wear all my baby dresses now?"

"Oh, Billie," says her dad, giving her a cuddle. "You should see him.

He's beautiful! And I'm sure he'll look lovely in your pretty pink dresses."

Billie giggles. "Where's Mom?" she asks. "Is she coming home now?"

"Not yet," her dad says. "Mom has to rest. She will be at the hospital for a few days. But we can go and see her."

"A few days!" Billie says crossly. "But I want Mom to come home now."

She **stamps** her foot.

Billie's dad sighs.

He thanks Jack's parents for taking care of Billie. Billie and her dad go back home for Billie to get dressed.

Billie feels all jumbled up inside. She is **excited** to see her new baby brother. But she also feels a teensy bit **cross** that he is a boy, not a girl.

She is **excited** to see her mom, but she is also **cross** that her mom is not coming home yet. All these feelings bubble up inside Billie's tummy like a milkshake.

Then she remembers.

"Mr. Fred!" she says. "I have to find Mr. Fred to give to the new baby!"

"OK," says her dad. "But quickly. Mom is waiting for us."

Billie looks everywhere for Mr. Fred. She looks under her bed. No Mr. Fred. Then she checks her toy box. Not there either!

She checks all the places Mr. Fred could be. But he is nowhere to be found.

"We have to go now," Billie's dad says. "We can give Mr. Fred to the baby next time."

"No!" says Billie. "I want Mr. Fred!" She **stamps** her feet.

"Billie!" says her dad. He is looking very tired. "Come on. You have to be a big girl now."

"But I don't want to be a big girl!" Billie cries. "I want to be a baby too!"

Billie's dad bends down and gives her a big hug.

"It's OK," he says gently. "You will always be my baby girl, Billie. Now how about we go see Mom?

We can look for Mr. Fred again when we get home."

Billie stops crying and gives her dad a big cuddle.

Chapter Four

Billie and her dad arrive at the hospital. Her mom is sitting up in bed. She holds out her arms and Billie jumps onto the bed for a cuddle.

Billie's mom points to a plastic crib next to the bed. "There's your little brother," she says. "His name is Noah. Isn't he adorable?"

Billie looks into the plastic crib. Noah is wrapped up like a fat white caterpillar. His face is all squishy and red. He doesn't look very adorable to Billie.

"Would you like to hold him?" her mom asks.

"Nah," says Billy snuggling up to her mom. "Maybe later."

Billie's mom lets her change the channels on the TV. Then Billie tells her mom about poor lost Mr. Fred.

Soon it is time to go. Billie kisses her mom goodbye. She even gives Noah a kiss. He smells nice. Like banana pancakes!

"Bye-bye, baby!" Billie says softly.

Just then Noah opens his eyes. He looks straight up at Billie. A little smile creeps over his tiny face. Then he closes his eyes again.

"He smiled at me!" Billie gasps.

"Wow, Billie! You're the first person he's smiled at," her mom says.

"That's because he knows you're his big sister," her dad says.

Billie feels very **proud**. She is the first person her baby brother has smiled at.

He likes her! Maybe it will be fun to be a big sister after all.

"OK, time to go," says her dad. "Let's go home and look for Mr. Fred, shall we?"

When they get home, Jack is waiting on Billie's front doorstep.

He has something in his arms. Something big and furry and wet and muddy.

"Mr. Fred!" Billie says.

"Oh dear," says her dad. "Did you leave him out in the rain?"

Billie nods. She gives poor old Mr. Fred a big cuddle.

She has missed him so much!

"I don't think I want to give Mr. Fred to Noah anymore," Billie says.

"After all, Mr. Fred is a bit old and dirty for our new baby."

Billie knows that being a big sister will be fun most days. But some days she might want to be a baby, too. She will need Mr. Fred on those days.

"But what will you give the baby?" Jack asks.

Billie smiles. "Our new baby needs a *new* teddy bear," she says. "Just for him!"

Then she giggles. "And do you know what else? I think Mr. Fred needs a bath!"

Billie B. Brown

The Spotty Vacation

Chapter One

Billie B. Brown has one package of mints, twelve colored pencils and a brand-new suitcase on wheels. Do you know what the "B" in Billie B. Brown stands for?

Bouncy.

Billie B. Brown is bouncing all over the place. She is as excited as a bunny! Do you know why Billie is so excited? She's going to stay with her grandma for a whole week!

Billie loves her grandma.

One package of mints

Twelve colored pencils

A brand-new suitcase on wheels

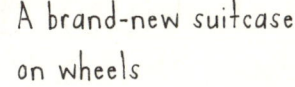

She lives in a city that is very far away. Too far away to drive. So Grandma is taking Billie there on a plane. How exciting!

On the plane, Grandma lets Billie sit by the window. Billie has never been on a plane before.

She wants to try all the buttons and games. She eats her whole package of mints before the plane even takes off.

"Billie," says her grandma. "How about you draw a picture or read a book?"

But Billie is too **excited** to draw or read. She has been counting sleeps for weeks!

When the plane takes off, it moves very fast and makes a loud noise. Billie is a teensy bit **scared**.

She peeks through the little window. The cars and houses outside get smaller and smaller below.

Billie has never seen anything so wonderful. It looks like fairyland! She's not scared anymore. But she squeezes Grandma's hand as they go through the clouds. **Bumpity bump bump**.

Billie has written a list of all the fun things they are going to do at Grandma's.

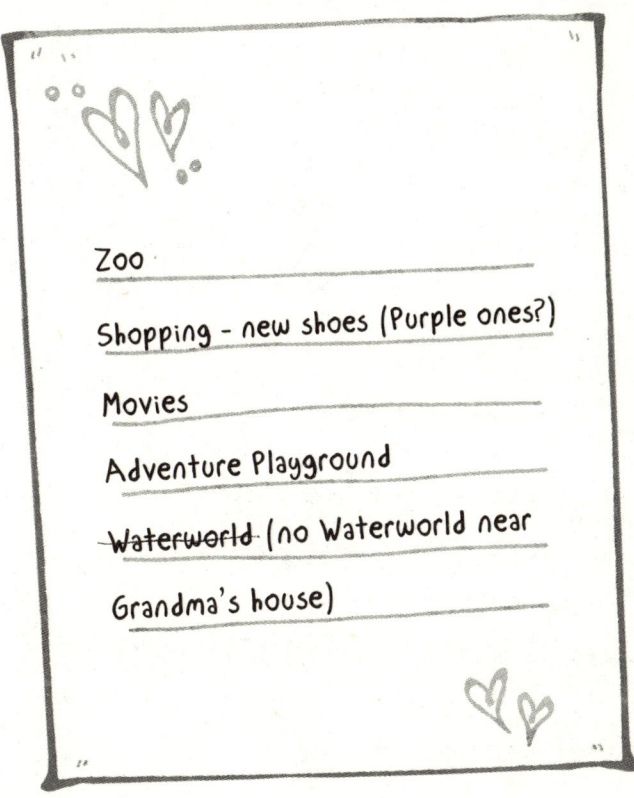

Billie can't *wait* until they get there. They have so much to do!

Chapter Two

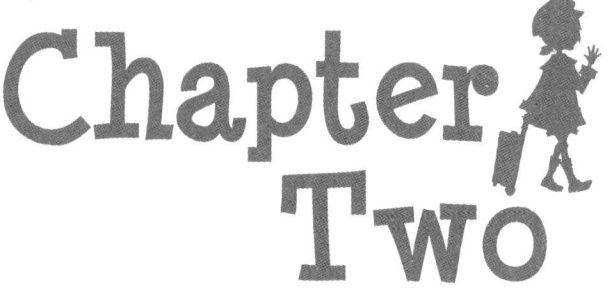

When they arrive at Grandma's apartment it is already dark.

Billie feels very tired. Grandma tucks Billie into a sofa bed in the study.

The sheets feel cool and crisp. But Billie feels **hot** and **itchy**. She has a bit of a tummy ache.

"Probably just all the excitement, love," Grandma says. She kisses Billie good night. "You'll feel better tomorrow."

Billie finds it very hard to get to sleep.

Grandma's apartment looks spooky in the dark. The traffic outside is very noisy! And Billie feels hotter and itchier than ever.

When Billie wakes up the next morning she is covered in spots. Do you know what they are? Chickenpox!

"Chickenpox?" says Billie.

"Chickenpox," says Grandma, shaking her head. "Luckily I've already had it so I can't catch it again.

But we don't want other children catching it. You'll have to stay inside until you are better."

"But what about the zoo?" Billie gasps. "And the movies? And my new shoes?"

Big fat tears roll down Billie's spotty cheeks.

"I'm sorry," sighs Grandma. "But there's nothing we can do. How about you get out your sketchbook and pencils? I'll make you breakfast in bed. French toast?"

"With banana?" Billie says, wiping her eyes.

"With banana," says Grandma.

Billie eats up all her breakfast. Then she calls her mom and dad.

"Guess what?" Billie's mom says. "Baby Noah has chickenpox, too!"

Billie laughs. She can't imagine her little brother all covered in spots.

"Hello, Noah!" Billie shouts down the phone.

After Billie says goodbye, she climbs back into bed and takes out her sketchbook and pencils.

But it's no use. She can't think of anything to draw.

Billie feels **itchy** and **scratchy** all over. Grandma says that Billie shouldn't scratch her spots or they will scar. Billie sighs. She wishes she could go outside to the park and the shops and the zoo.

Billie wrote so many fun things on her list and now she can't do any of them. What a miserable vacation!

Then, Billie has an idea. A super-duper idea!

You'll never guess what she is up to.

Chapter Three

"OK, Grandma," Billie calls. "You can come in now!"

Grandma walks into the family room. "Wow, Billie! This looks amazing," she says.

Billie giggles. Grandma is right. The family room looks…well, it doesn't look like a family room anymore.

Billie has been drawing pictures of zoo animals all morning. While Grandma made lunch, Billie stuck the pictures around the room.

She even moved some of Grandma's furniture to look like cages. Now the family room looks like a zoo!

Grandma and Billie walk around Billie's zoo looking at all the animals. "Be careful of that one!" Billie says. She points to Mr. Fred who is sitting in Grandma's laundry basket. "He's a ferocious bear!"

Grandma pretends to look scared. Billie laughs.

Grandma has packed a picnic for lunch. After they have seen all the animals, they sit down on the carpet to eat their sandwiches.

"How about we go to the ice cream shop next?" asks Grandma, winking.

"Yay!" says Billie following Grandma into the kitchen.

Grandma pretends to be the ice cream shop lady. She hands Billie a bowl of vanilla ice cream. Billie hands her some pretend money.

Then Grandma takes some things out of the cupboard. Bananas, chocolate chips, peanut butter, maple syrup and sprinkles.

"Would you like to choose a topping, madam?" she asks in a silly voice.

"Can I put anything on it?" Billie asks.

"Of course!" says Grandma.

Billie smiles. "Can I put *everything* on it?"

Grandma laughs. "Whatever you like, love."

Billie mixes everything into her ice cream until it is a big, goopy mess. Delicious! This vacation is much more fun than she thought.

That night after Billie's bath, Grandma puts a special cream on Billie's spots to stop them itching.

The spots are red and even itchier than before. But Billie is doing a very good job of not scratching them.

When Grandma has finished, Billie hops into bed and takes out her vacation list. She crosses out Zoo. What is next?

Shopping - new shoes.

Oh dear! How can they go shoe shopping when Billie has to stay inside? But then Billie has another idea. A super-duper idea. Even super-duperer than the last one!

Can you guess what she is thinking?

Chapter Four

The next morning Billie gets up early. There is so much to do!

"What's our plan for today?" Grandma asks over breakfast.

"Shoe shopping!" says Billie.

"Great," says Grandma. "I love shopping for shoes!"

Billie and Grandma go into Grandma's bedroom. Billie tries on all the shoes in the closet. Pink ones, sparkly ones, boots and sandals.

Finally Billie finds the perfect shoes. They are exactly the same purple as Billie's T-shirt. They are a teensy bit big, but Billie doesn't mind.

Billie and Grandma pay Mr. Fred, who is the shopkeeper.

Billie crosses Shopping - new shoes off her list.

"What's next?" asks Grandma.

"Going to the movies," says Billie.

"Hmm, OK," says Grandma.

"How about I ask my neighbor to pick us up some DVDs? We can make popcorn!"

"Yay!" says Billie. She jumps up and down in **excitement**.

"Glad to see you're still my bouncy Billie," says Grandma. "Even with the chickenpox!"

Billie makes movie tickets for herself and Grandma. Then she closes all the blinds in the family room so it is nice and dark. Just like at the movies!

When the theater is ready, she helps Grandma make popcorn in a big pan.

Billie loves watching the popcorn jump around inside the pan. **Pop pop pop!**

Billie and Grandma spend all week inside, but Billie never gets bored.

One morning Billie makes an adventure playground out of cushions. And that night she gets to play Waterworld – in the bathtub. What a mess!

On the last day of her vacation, Billie's spots have cleared up enough for her to go outside.

Which is lucky because it is time for Billie and Grandma to catch the plane home again.

On the plane, Billie fiddles with all the buttons on the armrest. She accidentally pushes the button to call the flight attendant.

"Oops, sorry!" says Billie when the woman arrives.

"That's all right, dear," says the attendant. She smiles at Billie and Grandma. "Are you on vacation with your grandma?"

"Yes," says Billie. "But I got the chickenpox so I couldn't go outside. We had to stay inside for a whole week!"

"Oh, what a shame," says the attendant. "That must have been a pretty boring vacation."

"No way," says Billie.

"We went to the zoo and ate ice cream. We went shopping and I even went to Waterworld!"

"Waterworld?" says the attendant. "But I thought you stayed at home?"

"We did," says Billie. "And I had the best vacation ever!"

The flight attendant looks confused.

But Billie and Grandma
look at each other
and giggle.

Collect them all!

 The Bad Butterfly
 The Soccer Star
 The Midnight Feast
 The Second-best Friend
 The Extra-special Helper

 The Beautiful Haircut
 The Big Sister
 The Spotty Vacation
 The Birthday Mix-up
 The Secret Message

 The Little Lie
 The Best Project
 The Deep End
 The Copycat Kid
 The Night Fright

 The Missing Tooth
 The Bully Buster
 The Grumpy Neighbor
 The Hat Parade
 The Honey Bees

 The Best Day Ever
 The Pocket Money Blues
 The Cutest Pet Ever

Don't forget the book starring both Jack AND Billie!
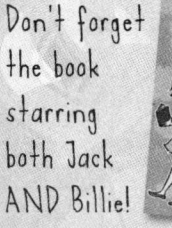